The Hole in the Wall

and Other Stories

Also by Floyd D. Norskog

Heartbeats
Flowers for Mom

Available on Amazon

The Hole in the Wall

and Other Stories

Floyd D. Norskog

Santa Rosa, California

Published by
Athena Star Press
2467 Westvale Court, Santa Rosa, California 95403, USA
http://athenastarpress.com

In association with
Old Paria Press
Floyd D. Norskog
13 West 750 South, Kanab, Utah 84741, USA

Cover art © Can Stock Photo / tolokonov

Many of the stories in this book are fiction or fictionalized versions of events that happened to the author or to other credible sources who told the author their stories. Characters, places, and incidents are the product of the author's imagination or are used fictitiously, and any resemblance to actual persons, living or dead, business establishments, events, or locale is entirely coincidental. The story about the ship the *General W. H. Gordon* is a true story. The story about faith healing in the Philippines is a true story as told to the author by his sister-in-law, Deanie Kelly.

Library of Congress Control Number: 2021948703
ISBN: 978-1-60038-002-0 (paperback)
First printing December 2021
Printed in the United States

Cover design by Marina Michaels
Interior design by Floyd Norskog and Marina Michaels
Edited by Marina Michaels

Dedication

This book is dedicated to my wife Ruth Elaine, my constant companion and motivation; my brother Lee Kelly and his wife Deanie; and my son-in-law and daughter, Thal and Kim Wright. Always there, giving advice, reading manuscripts, and giving encouragement. To my daughter, Marina Michaels. You made this book happen. You're a sweetheart and I love you dearly. As always, I am indebted to my mentors Liz Adair and Sylvia Newcomb. And to all the people I have ever known, you are also part of my writing.

Contents

The Hole in the Wall

ARTIN was frightened. There was a hole in the wall, and it was in his room. His new father was going to be terribly angry. Martin wasn't too sure he could fix it, and he didn't dare hang anything over it because his new father became angry if he so much as touched the walls. His only hope was that it wouldn't be noticed. Even if his new sister Jennifer had done it, it would probably be blamed on him.

After giving the hole much thought, he decided to pretend that he didn't see it. If he was lucky, his new father would not see it either and he would be all right. He was sure that he had not done it, and if asked would deny any involvement in it. Maybe his new father would just yell and turn red in the face but not hit him. Martin hated it when his new father hit him. Usually, he smacked him around and if he cried, he would yell at him. Martin usually just covered his head with his arms and tried not to cry out or shed tears. If he were lucky, the punishment would be over shortly, and things would settle back into a fragile normalcy.

When his new father had first come to live with them, things had been peaceful, but Martin missed his real father and cried a lot. Then the bed wetting had started, which led to the first time he was spanked. He just couldn't help it. Sometimes he stayed up all night to keep from doing it. Other times he slept in the bathtub, but was caught and was spanked for that also.

His mother was of little help, especially after Jennifer was born. She sided with his new father most of the time, or just ignored what was taking place. For a while he had his little dog Muffy for a friend, but even she was gone now. She had peed in the house and when he came home from school one day, Muffy was gone. All his mother would tell him was Muffy had gone to heaven and he would not see her again.

One morning Martin awoke to a great surprise. The hole in the wall had grown larger! Now he was in real trouble. His new father was sure to see it and punish him severely. Soon the boards the carpenters used to build the house would show and his new father would surely see it. Martin was almost sick. He lay in bed for a long time looking at the hole. Why did this have to happen to him? Why was he always in trouble? Now this.

Every day the hole in the wall become a little larger. Martin became more and more frightened. He was afraid his new father would send him wherever he sent Muffy. Martin was so frightened that he actually became sick. He was afraid to tell his mother he was ill, he was afraid of the hole in the wall, he just didn't know what to do. However, since the first time he had noticed the hole, when it was very tiny, his new father had said nothing about it. At first Martin was thankful for this, but soon, the very fact that his new father never saw it frightened him.

One morning Martin lay in bed looking at the hole. It was strange that he could not see the boards the builder used to build the house or the pink stuff they used to keep the cold out. Martin noticed the hole was gray and appeared to have smoke of some sort in it. If he listened very carefully, he could hear sounds far off in the distance coming from the hole.

Martin feared the hole as much as he feared his new father and tried not to go near it. One day after school as he played quietly in his room, he thought he heard Muffy whine. Martin thought that Muffy had come home and ran into the living room with a smile on his face.

"Stop running in the house," his new father shouted. "I've told you a thousand times not to run in the house. Now go to your room.

The next time I catch you running in the house, you will be punished."

Martin stopped dead in his tracks. Fear welled up in him as if he had been drenched with cold water, and he slunk back to his room. He had glanced around and had seen that Muffy was not there. He had been so sure that he had heard Muffy whine! He threw himself on his bed and buried his face in his pillow and cried.

The hole was now as big as the garbage can lid. It was near the end of the room between his little desk and toy box.

Martin had not gotten into his toy box for days for fear of being close to the hole. The only reason he worked at his little desk was because his new father insisted he sit there and do his homework every night. Martin tried to do exactly as he was told. The penalties were too high if there was a bad grade on his report card.

Martin woke to soft sounds in his room about a month after the hole first appeared. He looked at the little red numbers on his clock. It was 2:30 in the morning! He was lucky the sounds had wakened him. He needed to use the bathroom and would surely have wet the bed if he had not woken up. After quietly going to the bathroom so as to not wake up his new father, he crawled back under the blanket which were still warm with the heat from his body.

Martin lay in the dark listening to the strange sounds. They were just low enough so that he could not make out words. Occasionally he would hear a gentle laugh or a dog bark. Martin wondered if the dog could have been Muffy. The room was almost totally black except for the small red light given off by his clock. The corner of the room containing the hole was dark, except for the hole, which was a lighter shade of gray than the rest of the dark.

Finally, laying there in the dark, he drifted off to sleep. On the instant before dropping off to sleep, he thought he heard someone softly call his name. That night, he dreamed of his real father for the first time since he had died. His father was full of life again and they were walking in the woods with Muffy.

At school the next day, Martin was daydreaming about the hole and the soft sounds when he became aware that Mrs. Thompson was very angry at him. She had evidently called his name more than once and he had not responded. He hated her class anyway with all the numbers and the different things that he was supposed to do with them.

"I'm talking to you, young man!" she said sternly.

"Yes, ma'am?" Martin replied.

"We are picking up the homework, Martin! Where is yours?"

Martin's heart sank. His new father had been in an awfully bad mood that morning and in his haste to get out of the house, Martin had forgotten the homework.

"Well!" said Mrs. Thompson, in a slightly louder voice, "I expect an answer, Martin!"

"I forgot it," said Martin softly, "it's at home."

"What? What? Speak up, Martin, I can hardly hear what you are saying."

"Home," Martin said, in a slightly louder voice. "I left it at home."

"Well, well," said Mrs. Thompson again. "I think it's time I had a conference with your parents to see if we can determine why you are so inattentive in class and seem to never get your classroom work to school on time."

"No, no, Mrs. Thompson." Martin said in a panic. "I will do better. I will pay attention in class and I will turn in all my work on time. Please, Mrs. Thompson. Please."

"Well, we shall see. But this is the last time I am going to talk to you about this," she replied.

Martin breathed a great sigh of relief. Another crisis was past. He had to concentrate better in school. This was the second time that Mrs. Thompson had warned him, and he knew there would not be another time.

That evening Martin sat at his desk. His arithmetic book was open in front of him, but he was looking at the hole, which was to the left of his desk, between him and his toy box.

"What in the hell are you doing?" his new father screamed at him.

Martin nearly jumped out of his skin. He tried to look busy doing whatever it was he thought his new father wanted him to do, but a large, callused hand hit him in the back of the head, almost knocking him off his chair. Martin didn't have time to cry out before he was hit twice again, this time on the side of his head. His hands had gone up just in time to protect his ears.

"This is the third time I've come in here and told you to get busy and all you do is sit there and daydream."

The next blow hit Martin so hard that it knocked him from his chair. As he fell, he put out his arms to catch himself. In a brief instant he noticed that his hand had gone into the hole. He jerked it back and rolled into a ball away from the hole with his arms over his head.

"One more time," his new father shouted, his face red with anger, "and I will teach you a lesson you won't forget. Do you understand?" he screamed. He grabbed Martin by the hair and lifted him partly off the floor.

Martin was so frightened he could hardly move but he did manage to shake his head yes. His mother and Jennifer stood in the doorway watching. His mother made no effort to help him. Jennifer had a small smirk on her face. Martin waited for the next blow, but it never came.

After a few moments, his new father let him go and he slumped back on the floor.

"Now get up and get to work! And I don't want to have to tell you again!"

Martin scrambled to get back into his chair and still maintain a safe distance in case his new father took a notion to smack him again. Tears streamed down his face, and he kept it turned away from the rest of the family so they wouldn't see them. Martin wanted desperately to look at his hand closely and be sure it was not hurt in some way, but he didn't dare. He fumbled with his books and attempted to look busy. After a few minutes everybody left. Later, when he was sure he was alone, Martin scrutinized his hand carefully. As near as he could tell, there was no visible damage. A seed of curiosity about the hole begin to grow inside of him.

The next day on the way to school, he heard someone call to him.

"Hey, Skinny, doesn't your mother have any clothes that fit you?"

Martin looked back. The DeWitt kids from the next block over were following him. There were two brothers and a sister, within a few years of being his age. Their clothes were dirty and ill-fitting and they seldom bathed. They had a reputation of tormenting other kids, but to date had not bothered Martin. He thought the best thing to do was walk on and ignore them.

Soon they were on both sides of him. The sister poked at him with a stick and one of the brothers was picking at his clothes. Suddenly, the sister stuck the stick between his legs and down he went. He was more frightened than hurt, but tears came to his eyes.

"What's the matter with the little baby?" one brother laughed. "Does she want a sugar tit?"

"He doesn't like his pants. They don't fit. Let's take them off for him," said the other brother.

Martin was mortified. He had never had a girl see him with his pants off. The sister, the youngest of the threesome, smiled as both brothers jumped on him, pinning him to the ground. Martin was beside himself. Adrenaline surged through his body and he managed to push one brother off and shake free of the other. He ran down the street as fast as he could go. Peals of laughter followed him.

"We'll get you after class!" one of them shouted.

Martin was terrified. He didn't see how he could go to class, and he didn't see how he could go home. However, if he didn't go to class, his new father would find out eventually and there would be trouble at home. If he did go to school, the DeWitt kids would get him. Martin wandered in the woods and streets until it was time to go home. He went home at the usual time and went straight to his room and pretended to study as usual. He tried to ignore the hole in the wall.

Martin lay in bed that night trying to figure out what he could do. The teacher would certainly demand a note from his mother if he went back to school. He might be able to fake the note, but eventually his mother would find out. Besides, there was still the problem with the DeWitt kids if he did go back to school. Surely, they had decided he was good bait for their practical jokes, and next time he might not be so lucky.

As he lay there pondering his dilemma, he heard a voice. At first, he couldn't make it out, but soon he decided someone was calling his name. He tried to keep his breathing as quiet as possible so he could understand the words. He was sure he had heard the word "Martin." Perhaps Jennifer was playing tricks on him. It was very dark in his room and Jennifer was afraid of the dark, so it probably wasn't her. Martin heard someone laugh and a dog bark. Then he heard the voice again.

"Martin. Martin. Are you there?"

Martin slipped out of bed and moved closer to the hole. Just closer. Not near enough to touch it though. He listened intently.

"Martin. Do you hear me buddy? It's me, Dad."

It sounded like his real dad. He wanted to believe it was. But he wasn't sure, and he was frightened. He sat there quietly and listened. The laughing continued and he was sure that the barking he heard was Muffy. If only it were true, he thought.

"Come over here, buddy," the voice said. "Don't be afraid. Look through the hole and tell me what you see."

Martin leaned closer and peered into the hole. At first all he could see was the swirling mist, but as he looked closer, he could make out what appeared to be a city park. He could make out swings and a slide. It was strange, for the sun was shining. As he looked closer, he could see people and a dog. Martin felt strangely excited.

"Is that really you, Daddy?" he said.

"Yes," the voice replied, "come over here and play ball with me and Muffy."

"I'm scared."

"It's okay, buddy. Just crawl through and come to my voice."

Martin found that the fog that was in the hole would not hurt him. It felt slightly cool, and when he had put his hand in, he had felt no pain. Maybe if he talked to his real Dad, his real Dad could help him solve his problems. He reached out and stuck his hand into the hole and quickly jerked it out. He had felt nothing. He stuck it in a second time as far as he could. Still there was no pain. Martin tentatively crawled into the hole. After he had gone a little way, he could see the playground plainly. He stood up and walked toward the swings. He saw his real father, tall and lean, with a baseball mitt on one hand and a ball in the other.

"Hey! Catch!" his father called.

He tossed the ball under hand to Martin. Martin was so surprised to see him, he just let the ball hit him in the chest and drop to the ground. Then he spotted Muffy running toward him. He dropped down on his knees and threw his arms around him. Muffy whined and licked his face. Martin was so excited he was crying.

"Hey! Throw the ball back!" His father laughed.

Martin picked up the ball and ran to his father and threw his arms around him. He was really crying now.

"All right now, that's enough. You look like a boy who could use some ice cream. Let's say me and you go get some."

"And Muffy?"

"Yes, and Muffy." His father laughed and took him by the hand and led him to the truck at the edge of the park. Muffy ran alongside of them. Martin had so many things to talk to his father about. So many questions. But they could all wait. He had not been this happy in a long time.

Epilog

The doctor sent Martin's parents out of the room. He sat in a hard-backed chair beside the bed. Martin had not moved in the two or three hours he had been there. He lay flat on his back with his eyes open. The doctor had checked him for obvious abuse and the results were inconclusive. Martin's parents appeared to be normal, everyday parents, and seemed genuinely concerned. He looked around the room. It was neat and clean with a bed, a closet, a little study desk, and a toy box. The walls were covered with wallpaper depicting race cars.

Maybe shock treatment, he thought. Or there were some new drugs.

He would talk to Martin's parents and decide on a plan of treatment.

Far off, in the distance, he heard a dog barking.

Endangered Species

FRANK woke slowly, his eyes closed, only slightly aware of his location. His stomach was upset, and his head buzzed as if he had a hangover or had slept too long. He kept his eyes closed, as he often did when he was unsure where he was, and tried to analyze his situation. His right hand moved to the right, testing, but there was no one in bed with him. Where he was, was comfortably warm, and he could detect daylight through his eyelids. With the end of this preliminary search, he opened his eyes.

The room was spacious, with windows in the two intersecting walls. The bed was king size, with an attractive covering, albeit somewhat dirty. An end table with a couch was to his immediate right, and beyond that a small kitchenette. Down a hall, he could see a room he supposed to be a bathroom. To his left, through sliding glass doors, he could see a volleyball court and trees on a sharp slope which blocked the rest of his vision. Directly across from him was a writing desk, a vanity with a television on it, and a closet.

He had never in his life been in this room to his knowledge.

Where the hell am I? he thought.

He hadn't moved except for opening his eyes since awakening. Out of the corner of his eye, between the foot of the bed and the sliding glass doors, there was a pile of what looked like clothes. As he moved slightly, he saw a bare foot on the floor. He allowed himself to lie back and close his eyes again.

"Where the hell am I?" he asked himself again.

By this time, he was more than a little frightened.

Very carefully he began evaluating his actions of the night before. He remembered coming home drunk, again, and Millie being extremely angry, again. He had yelled at her, saying unforgivable things, and stalked out, walking back toward town. After another hour of heavy drinking, he had started home again when the bars closed. However, as he approached his house, he decided to walk for a while and clear his head.

The night had been cool, and the lights of the small village fell away behind him quickly. The moon was almost full and as his eyes acclimated to the available light he could see quite well. He remembered the beauty of the Milky Way and the enormity of the Big Dipper. His ears had become accustomed to the quiet and he could hear crickets and other night sounds. That is where it ended. Abruptly. He could remember nothing of the night after that.

Now this. Who was on the floor? Had he gone home with someone at some point in the night? Had he somehow hurt someone in a drunken rage?

Dear God, he thought, don't let it be that.

He had never struck Millie. Actually, he had never struck anyone. He was not a violent person and was quite sure he hadn't hurt anyone. However, who was that on the floor? He was going to have to face things before too long, so it had might as well be now.

He moved just enough to see the foot. He looked at it intently. It was tanned and the ankle was slim. It was also quite dirty. From the size, he was quite sure it was a woman's foot. Very carefully he raised himself on his elbow for a better view.

It was a woman, and a quite young woman, perhaps half his age. She was dressed in a simple smock-like dress and there was not a shoe on the other foot either. Her hair was tangled and dirty. A blanket covered part of her body, and what he could see was moderately attractive. She wore no makeup, and her eyes were closed. Her breast rose and fell with her soft breathing. He was relieved to see she appeared unhurt.

Here goes, he thought, and sat up in the bed.

The young woman let out a frightened cry. She rose in a kneeling position, her eyes big and frantic, and started backing toward the sliding glass doors, which were partially open.

He opened his mouth to say something, but before he could, she backed out the doors and, holding the blanket around her, raced across the volleyball court, and disappeared into the trees out of sight. It all happened so suddenly, he had little time to react. He sat there in the bed with his mouth open. When he realized his mouth was open, he shut it.

"Goddamn," he said.

He got out of the bed and explored the building. The room down the hall turned out to be a bathroom, as he had suspected. There were clean towels, shaving equipment, toothbrush and toothpaste. He had never seen any of it before and none of the toothpaste and shaving lotion was a brand that he would have bought. The facilities were in slight disarray and messy without being dirty. Back in the living part of the quarters, the stove worked, as did the refrigerator. There was food in the refrigerator. He found dishes in the cupboards, coffee, and a coffee maker in the cabinet beneath the sink.

What the hell, he thought. I might as well have some coffee. Morning coffee had always been Millie's job, but he thought he could figure it out.

He filled the coffee basket, guessing on how much coffee to use, and added water to the percolator. As he waited, he searched his clothes for a cigarette. He eventually found a rumpled pack in the inside pocket of his sport jacket. Unfortunately, there were no matches. He had to use the flame from the gas stove for a light. The smoke tended to settle him by the second or third drag, but he still had a craving for a "morning after" drink. As soon as he got his wits about him, he would get the hell out of wherever he was, get a drink, and see about getting back home.

The smell of the coffee bought back memories of other mornings and other places, and Millie. Millie would be mad as hell at him for staying out all night. Maybe he should slow down a little on the booze and try to be a little nicer to her. Maybe buy her something nice. In the days when they were newlyweds, he could always get her to smile and get her into a loving mood. Now she seldom talked to him except to chew on him for drinking or staying out late. She was, really, an exceptionally good old girl. They had been together for more than twenty years now. He could not imagine being without her. Deep in his heart he knew he loved her and should be a better husband.

The first thing he had to do was to find out where he was so he could get back home. The girl bothered him somewhat, but it really was not his problem. Millie was his problem and he had to get home and do some damage control. The girl would just have to look out after herself. Maybe later, when the dust had settled, he would try to figure that one out.

He drank some more of the coffee, which was slightly weak, then washed his hands and face. He felt a little better and decided to do some looking around. Once outside, he realized where he had slept was a small cabin. It was surrounded by a well-manicured lawn and a few trees. A paved road ran in front of it, and he could see it turn in the distance. No other roads were visible, and no other buildings were in sight. For some reason, his watch had stopped operating. Judging from the sun, the time was ten or eleven o'clock.

He chose an arbitrary direction and started down the road. The sun was warm, and he whistled tunelessly to himself. It was a nice day, and the sun would burn the remainder of the alcohol out of him. As he walked, he scanned the low brush and few trees that lined the road.

For no apparent reason he become lightheaded. As he walked further, the lightheadedness increased to a buzzing and finally a full-blown migraine.

Christ! he thought to himself, Maybe I should go back to the cabin and lay down for an hour.

He turned and started back toward the cabin. By now the migraine was worse and he staggered slightly. After a few steps, the migraine abated, and within another twenty feet had disappeared entirely. He stopped and looked around. He suddenly felt fine. He looked down the road in the direction from which he had come, and everything was the same, except he felt fine now.

"That's strange," he mused. "I feel fine. That booze is doing funny things."

As he started back down the road in the direction he had been going, the same thing happened. After a few steps he become lightheaded again and the further he went, the worse his head hurt. He immediately turned and went back toward the cabin. Again, within twenty feet he felt fine.

"Something is not right here," he said aloud.

He turned again and stared down the road the direction he was going. Everything seemed normal. He walked off the road into the brush. Whenever he started becoming lightheaded, he moved closer to the cabin. It had become apparent that if he had gone a certain distance from the cabin, the headaches started. He estimated that whenever he got over a half a mile from the cabin, the headaches started. All morning he tested his theory. Different directions from the cabin produced the same effect. He was effectively in a prison with the cabin as a center.

In all this time he had not seen another living thing. Not the girl, a bird, a rabbit, nothing.

He returned to the cabin and found a colored bedsheet. He tore it into small strips, and this time as he walked the perimeter around the cabin, he tied a small strip of cloth to a bush or a tree every hundred yards or so, thus marking his prison. By the time he was finished, the sun was starting to set, and he realized he was hungry.

Returning to the cabin, he took food from the refrigerator and attempted to cook himself something to eat. There was a package of hamburger in the freezer compartment that was as hard as a rock, and he realized it would not be his meal for the night. However, there were two medium-size steaks in the cooler portion, and some potatoes. He put the steaks on a low heat, washed and sliced the potatoes, skins and all, and started them frying in a second frying pan. After a careful search, he discovered a can of corn, which he opened and put to heat in a small sauce pan that was available.

God, how he wished Millie were here. She could make a meal out of almost anything. And make it good, too. He was not a cook, and things were beginning to burn. He lowered the heat, turned the meat, and mixed the potatoes a little. The corn boiled over, and he was so busy he didn't see the girl come in through the sliding doors.

When he looked at her, she cowered and prepared to run again.

"I'm not going to hurt you," he said. "Why don't you eat a little with me? Then we will figure out together where the hell we are." He took a cautious step toward her.

In an instant she was gone again.

Thoughtfully he finished cooking the meal. He prepared a plate and placed it on the back porch for the girl. After eating, he straightened up the room. Finally, he checked the food on the plate on the back porch. It was gone and the girl was nowhere to be seen.

In the days that followed, he settled into a routine. He did the cooking for both him and the girl. She ate on the porch and he seldom saw her. Occasionally she slept in the cabin with him. If he awakened in the night and the sliding doors were open, he knew she was there. He was a late sleeper, and he seldom saw her in the morning.

One morning he woke to find fresh food in the refrigerator and a change of clothes for the two of them. Somehow, whoever was keeping them there had left the items. He had not wakened in the night and could not figure how the material had gotten there. Whoever it was must have come through the "mind field," as he called it. If they could create it, they probably could turn it off. He concluded he was being watched and was starting to become paranoid. He would sit for hours watching the perimeter for some kind of a movement. He searched every inch of the compound for something other than plant life and found none. He double-checked the perimeter for any variances in the area that was allotted to him. He searched the cabin from front to back. He found absolutely nothing.

Analyzing his situation, he concluded that he and the girl were the only animals in the isolated compound. It was impossible to leave the compound. Something was caring for them and providing their necessities. Beyond that, he was at a loss. He found various places in the compound where the girl stayed when she didn't stay in the cabin. It had been warm, and he was sure she had a blanket or something to keep herself covered. The important question was, how was he going to get back home? Secondarily, why was he here in the first place?

He had tried to keep track of the number of days that he had been there. He had reached the point that he had to get out of there. He had attempted to rush the "mind field" that surrounded the compound but had fainted from the pain. When he awoke, he was back in his bed. He had no recollection of being taken there. He had thought maybe the girl had put him there, but he doubted it. But if not her, then who?

Finally, he decided on a plan. He would start a fire, and when whoever kept him captive came to put it out, he would make his escape. He worried about the girl, but there was little he could do about her. In all the time he had been there. they hadn't exchanged so much as a word. He had slowly moved her dish so she would eat just inside the door if he stayed on the other side of the room.

He found a more secluded part of his prison and started making a pile of flammable debris. It was carefully hidden in some of the denser brush. When evening came, he would set it on fire and try to discern where his captors came into his prison.

Upon returning to the cabin, he discovered the bedding had been changed and a new supply of food had been provided. Over a fresh pot of coffee, he considered these new findings. He had been outside for about three hours and had not kept a close watch on the cabin. Of course, someone could have entered from the outside without him noticing, but it was more likely that the cabin was entered through some sort of passage within the cabin itself. He carefully thought this over. The incident shed new light on his predicament. After giving it a good deal of thought, he decided to go ahead with the fire that night, and later search the cabin from top to bottom if nothing worked out with the fire.

He looked up, noticing the girl watching him intently from the patio doors. He saucered a cup of coffee and, walking slowly, placed it on the corner of the bed. After he had retreated to the far end of the cabin, the girl stepped in and took the cup of coffee and withdrew to the far corner of the bed. Holding the coffee cup in both hands, she watched him intently.

"I'm making a diversion tonight," he told her. "When the fire starts, we will have to be on our toes and find where they enter the compound and how they do it. If it looks like a chance to escape, we'll do it. You're on your own. If you choose to stay with me, I'll try to protect you."

She watched him over the edge of her coffee cup, but he could see no indication that she understood him. Her eyes seemed alert but uncomprehending. She watched for a short while longer, then slipped out through the patio doors.

The two of them would have a better chance of getting out. He had, however, concluded that there was something mentally wrong with her. He had yet to hear her speak, except for guttural declarations, sounds of surprise or fear, and a soft singsong keening. It was too bad, but if need be, he would have to leave her. Later, if he got out and was clear, he would somehow try to get back and rescue her. Right now, his primary concern had to be keeping his wits about him and getting out.

When night fell, he turned on the lights in the front part of the cabin and pretended to doze on the couch. He went to bed, turning the lights entirely out. Later, he arose, and lit one of his cotton socks on fire from the stove. When it was burning brightly, he blew it out, creating a smoking pile of embers. Shielding it carefully, he slipped out through the sliding glass doors and around the building. With his heart hammering, he ran quickly to the pile of debris he had made earlier in the day. Burying the sock under the edge with the smallest tinder, he blew on it until he had a flame. Within moments, the pile was an inferno. He stepped back to admire his handiwork.

Within moments, he heard a loud humming and, from what he had deduced was the east, an aircraft approached him. It was shaped like a First World War soldier's helmet and was large enough to carry three or four humans. A small door opened. A slender pipe emerged from the door and pointed directly at him. He was too dumbfounded to move. As he stood there transfixed, a narrow beam of blue light moved toward him from the pipe. Before he could move, his head started buzzing, and he passed out.

When he became conscious, he was back in the cabin and he smelled slightly of singed hair and smoke.

I need you, Millie, he thought.

Suddenly he was afraid. He was no closer to determining where he was than he was the day he had found himself here.

The girl was nowhere to be seen. When daylight came, he would cook some breakfast and see if she showed up as she usually did.

Until then, the catastrophe with the blue light had not discouraged him. He was getting out of the damn place one way or other.

Communication with the girl might give him some answers. He had thought she might have had some sort of intellectual disability or suffered a breakdown being here, but now he wasn't sure. She had been at the fire, and he was quite sure if he could have made a break for it, she would have followed.

There was something out there somewhere watching and monitoring everything he did. He was sure of that now. He wondered how their night vision was. Where were they watching him from, he pondered? Was there some way they could be blinded? The fire trick had obviously not worked. What would he try next?

A tunnel might be an idea and, although it was long term, he felt he should get it started while he was trying to work out some other idea. Also, he didn't know whethr the field that affected his mind would not penetrate the ground also.

The sky was turning light, announcing another day, but the man had drifted off to sleep as plans of escape worked themselves through his mind.

Somewhere in the myriad of stars that make up the Milky Way, a message is transmitted. Loosely translated, it reads:

Memo

From: Director of Endangered Species Project
To: Commandant of the Federation of Milky Way Worlds
Subj: Status of Homo Sapiens Project

Due to the violence exhibited by the male of the species, it has been decided to abandon the project and return the subjects to their original planets.

End of message

When he awoke, he sat up and carefully ran his hands through his hair. Dawn was breaking and the sky to the East was lighter than the blackness overhead. He tried to get to his feet, but was overcome with a wave of nausea. Sitting back down, he hung his head between his knees until the feeling passed. Again, he tried to rise to his feet. This time he made it by holding on to the limb of a tree nearby. The longer he stood, the more stable he became.

He suddenly realized he was at the side of the road near his home.

He walked toward the house on the hill he shared with Millie. Thoughts of the fire, the cabin, and the girl fluttered through his head. In the distance, a light came on and he realized it was his house.

"This is going to be tough," he told himself. Millie was definitely going to be mad. She might not even allow him in the house, but he had no place left to go. The incidents of the last weeks had left him exhausted, and all he wanted to do was make peace with Millie and lie down for a while. Somewhere along the line he would have to find the courage to explain it all to her.

He stopped when he reached the back door and watched through the window as Millie worked at the stove. The old feelings washed over him and his happiness at finally being home gave him courage to open the door.

Millie would not even look at him. He approached the stove and retrieved a cup from the table. She turned, watching him with one hand on her hip and the other one hanging by her side. Her face was expressionless, and the anger radiated from her like heat. Feeling an explosion was eminent, he spoke first.

"Millie—" he started.

With her free hand, she struck the table, nearly startling him out of his wits.

"Don't 'Millie' me! Don't even *talk* to me! Damn you! Damn you!"

Millie seldom ever swore. He was shocked and raised one hand to calm her, but she refused to allow him to speak.

"This is the last time! I've tolerated this for twenty years! Either you're my husband or you're not. Make up your mind. Other wives' husbands don't stay out all night on drunken binges! Other wives don't get sworn at like dogs! This is it, Frank! And I mean it! You straighten up or we are through!"

"Millie—" he started again, but something she had said was stuck in his mind and he couldn't quite put his finger on it. Something wasn't exactly right.

"I've cleaned for you, I've fed you, I've worked for rich ladies so our kids would have nice clothes on their backs and the rent would be paid. Last night I decided this was the end of it. I wasn't taking it anymore."

There it was again. Something she was saying just wasn't right. She was mad, but she was mad for the wrong reason somehow.

He frowned. "Millie," he said, "listen to me."

"You're filthy," she answered. "There is dirt and leaves in your hair and your clothes are grubby! Where did you sleep last night?"

That was it! She had said "last night." What did she mean "last night?" What was going on here? Suddenly it dawned on him. The weeks in the cabin had been erased. How was he ever going to be able to explain it to her? How was he ever going to explain it to anybody? The thought crossed his mind that maybe it never really happened. But he knew it had. Where had he been? Where was the cabin and the girl? Where was that force that had so effectively kept him prisoner?

He got up and walked out the screen door and stood on the porch. The dayglow was gone from the east and the entire sky was now bright. He looked up and wondered. Who could he tell? Who would believe him?

He went back in the house, walked up behind Millie, and put his arms around her. She struggled momentarily, then stood silent. He kissed her hair and then kissed the nape of her neck.

"You will never know what you mean to me," he said. He held her like that so she couldn't see the tears on his cheeks.

Going Away

S HE listened for the train. It was going to be late, and her nerves were on edge. Denny stood away from her to her left, still reading the letter. She and Denny had been inseparable since she had moved back from the farm. Last year he had been the first boy to ever kiss her. Finally, the hand holding the letter dropped to his side.

"I don't understand. Why do you have to be the one that goes?" he pouted. "Your mom could go, or someone there could look after her. Doesn't she have friends there? Isn't there agencies that do things like that?"

"No," she said. "My mom can't go. She has to work." Why couldn't he understand that it was a choice she had made after much thought? That it was important to her that he understand her actions? "Grams can't care for herself since the accident," she added. "Granddad has to look after the farm. He works daylight to dark just to make ends meet!"

She thought of Grams and Granddad. She had lived with them on the farm in North Dakota for two years after her dad had left. Her mother had gone back to school and finished her degree so she could support them. She could see the barns and the house with their weathered gray-white boards. She could see Grams in her flowered apron holding a dish towel. A smile played on her lips. She thought of Pal and could imagine his happy bark when he saw her get off the train.

"She needs me, Denny. When I needed them, they were there, and now it is my turn. It's my idea to go. It would just be too hard with a stranger in the house."

In the distance, she could hear the train. Finally! She would be glad when it was there and she was gone. Denny was not making things any easier. She thought of her friends at school and how much she enjoyed being there.

As if reading her mind, Denny spoke again.

"What about school? What about all your friends? You're only 16. This is a job for adults! I don't see why you have to be the one to do it."

She turned and looked at him. "Dennis, people do things for different reasons. Sometimes they do things because it pleases them. Sometimes they do things to please someone else. Sometimes they do things because they think it is the right thing to do. I think this is the right thing to do." She never called him Dennis unless she was really irritated with him.

"I won't wait. If that's all you think of me, I'll find another girl," Denny whined.

The train pulled into the station with a screech of brakes and the blare of a whistle. Tears burned her eyes as she picked up her suitcase. She turned so Denny could not see them and walked down the station platform to the waiting Pullman car.

She didn't look back.

Oswan
and How the Navajo
Came to Have Dogs

BEFORE the time of written words, when language was still written in pictures, and before the white people came to the Americas, one of the First Nations peoples, the Navajo, lived in what is now the American southwest. The Navajo were and are a peaceful people, living on crops from their fields and wool and meat from their flocks of sheep.

Dogs did not exist during those early times. Herders had goats and the male sheep (called rams) to help them guard the sheep. This was well, but the coyote was crafty and able to steal many lambs from the herders despite the goats and rams. This caused much hardship for the Navajo, and many were the days that they were forced to eat only corn and squash from their fields. If the rains did not come, the Navajos would sit around their fires with empty stomachs.

During this time, there was a mother coyote who lived in an earthen den beneath a twisted pinyon tree. Here she had given birth to a litter of three pups. The two male pups were normal, but the third pup, though quite normal in most respects, was a little strange in other ways. All three loved to follow their mother and learn the things that coyotes should know. She taught them to how to hunt mice and rabbits and other small rodents that lived in the desert. She taught them what plants to eat when they were sick and to lick their wounds when they were hurt so the wound would heal.

She also taught them how to get the Navajo's newborn lambs. She taught them to be careful of the goats and the rams that helped the herder guard the sheep. She also taught them that the herders would kill them if they could, especially if they were near the sheep. However, even with the goats and the rams and the herders, it wasn't hard for the clever coyote to catch the fat baby lambs and eat them.

This is where the third coyote pup, Oswan, was different. She liked the herders and respected the sheep. At night she would creep up close to their fires and listen to them talk amongst themselves and tell their stories. She found she could learn the meaning of their words by listening carefully and watching.

They would talk about the coyotes killing the newborn lambs and how hard it was to guard them. They spoke of their families not having enough to eat because of the losses of the lambs. They talked of how lonely it was on the desert. This made Oswan incredibly sad. She knew what it was like to have her tummy growl with hunger and the long hours on the desert.

One day she decided she would walk right up to the fire and tell the herders how she felt. She would tell them how she longed to be their friend and how she would help them guard the sheep. So, after much thought, she walked right up to their campfire. She wanted to say, "I want to be your friend, and I won't hurt your sheep."

What she actually said was, "Arf! Arf! Bark! Bark!"

The startled herders chased her away. They were very surprised and angry, and she barely escaped with her life.

It came to her that she had a really big problem. She could understand the Navajo's language, but she could not speak it, and the Navajos could not understand coyote talk at all. Oswan went to her mother and asked her what she should do. Her mother was disappointed that Oswan wanted to do this, but she told her if it was really what she wanted to do, Oswan should go to Old Coyote, the oldest coyote in the land, and ask him for advice.

So Oswan went to the Old Coyote and asked him what she should do.

The old coyote had never in his life heard such a request. For a long time, he sat, looking out across the desert as the sun slowly set. He did not have an answer for the young female. Truly, he thought, the elder of the Navajos was the only one that could solve Oswan's problem.

Old Coyote said, "If this is your true wish, you must go to the great Shaman of the Navajo. You must sit quietly in front of him and look into his eyes. If you wait long enough, he will know all that is in your heart, and he will tell you what to do."

So Oswan went to the old Navajo Shaman and sat in front of him, with her ears up and her big bushy tail wrapped around her feet. She was very frightened. The old Navajo Shaman was startled to see the young coyote sitting in front of him. Somehow, he knew the coyote meant him no harm. He looked into Oswan's big brown eyes and she looked into his. Long into the night they sat like this, staring at each other over the flickering fire.

Finally, the words in Oswan's heart flowed into the old man's soul and the old man understood the words the little coyote longed to tell him. After much thought, the old man told Oswan she could forever be a friend of the Navajo's if that were truly her wish, but he would have to change her so the herders could tell her from the coyotes.

Little Oswan was shocked, and she said, "But I love my strong legs and my sharp teeth. I don't want to lose my ears that enable me to hear so well or my eyes that allow me to see in the dark. I love my bushy tail that keeps me warm in the long night. Must I give all this up?"

The old man smiled his toothless smile and his eyes sparkled. He said, "You will have all of these, only better and somewhat different. Man will always be able to tell you from the coyotes. He will feed and care for you and love you. You will reward him by loving and protecting him and his family and guarding his sheep. Your new name will be 'dog,' and you will always live with the Navajo."

He raised his old hand, and what he said was so. Oswan's body become stout, and her legs became powerful. Her head was broader, and her nose was blunter. Her fangs were sharper, and her jaws were stronger. Her coat became a different color. The Navajo would never mistake her for the small, gray coyote again. Finally, the great Shaman of the Navajos placed the seeds inside of her that would later become six new puppies just like her. They would also grow to be large, powerful dogs and friends to the Navajo. Oswan went to her mother and her brothers and said, "I am now dog and the friend of the Navajo. Though you are my mother and my siblings, you must never bother the sheep again. If you come to bother the sheep, I will chase you away."

And so it came to be from that day on that dog and her progeny would forever guard the sheep and protect and love the Navajo families. In return, the Navajo fed the dog and gave them friendship and allowed them to sleep by their fire. Times were good and the Navajo were seldom hungry. To this day, the dog lives with the Navajo and guards their sheep.

Author's Note

No one knows how the Navajo came to have dogs. This secret is hidden in the shrouds of time. The author researched Navajo stories, but found nothing to give him a clue. The story came to the author in the dark of night when he couldn't sleep, so he passes it on to you.

The Death of John Doe

I N the 1960s, Clayton Memorial Hospital was in the rolling country of the American Midwest, a large, ugly assortment of dreary gray buildings. It was a state hospital for the mentally ill, both civil and criminal. The grounds consisted of seven units arranged in a semicircle, with an opening to accommodate a blacktop road that eventually led to the interstate.

As one entered the hospital grounds, the nurses and employee quarters were in the first building on the right. The next four buildings were for civil patients (those not sent there for a criminal offense), and included male and female wards, laundry, dining rooms, cafeteria, store, and other facilities of a small city.

Administration was on the ground floor of the sixth building, and female criminal inmates were on the upper floors of this building. The seventh building, where I worked and ultimately met John Doe, was where male patients serving time or awaiting sentence for crimes were housed. These patients were serving time for various crimes. Some came directly from the courts, others were transferred from various prisons throughout the state when it became apparent their mental condition had deteriorated to the point they could no longer function in the prison environment.

This building, referred to as the Male Security Building, was shaped like a semicircle, with the ends of the circle connected by a two-story high brick wall, the space inside forming the recreation yard. Inside, the building was divided into wards, dining rooms, recreation rooms, doctor's offices, and all the other necessary amenities to make itself self-supporting.

Each ward was designed for a special function. For example, nine wards were the release ward. Patients had separate rooms, like a small hotel. By contrast, ward 7A was a maximum-security ward, with double interlocking doors to enter, and the patients were in separate cells. There was a ward for mentally ill teenagers, an old man ward, a hospital ward for those too ill to be in the general population, and everything in between.

The staff that worked there were called Psychiatric Aides, not guards or jailers. The person in charge of the ward for a particular shift was called the Charge Aide. A ward might have one to four or more Aides to support the operation of the ward depending on the needs of that ward, such as the number of patients on a ward, how violent they were, etc. At the time of this story, early 1961, I was the Charge Aide on the hospital ward. It was here that I first met John Doe.

"Hospital Ward," in this case, was a little bit of a misnomer. We did have patients that were confined to bed, but most were just people who needed extra care. There was Ivan, who had been shot by a police officer and was paralyzed from the waist down. Then there was Andy, an epileptic who had seizures so severe he wore a football helmet all the time to keep from hurting himself. There were others with bad hearts, crippled with arthritis, and similar ailments. These patients did not fit well with the general institution population due to unavoidable violence on wards housing younger men.

Then there was John.

John had been picked up on some kind of charge in a nearby city. He was homeless, and street people, especially those with mental problems, tend to be frightening to the general population. People accuse them of a crime, and because they can't defend themselves, eventually, guilty or innocent, they ended up in institutions such as Clayton Memorial Hospital.

John didn't know his name or his age. While awaiting records from the FBI and various other sources, he was given the name of John Doe. No record was ever found of him or his fingerprints and the name just stuck.

John stood almost six feet tall and weighed maybe one hundred fifty pounds. He had all his hair, which was gray, and he let it hang randomly like loosely stacked straw. The doctors thought he might be in his late fifties or early sixties. He was meticulous about himself and kept his body and clothes clean. He had a pale dead look in his eyes that never changed unless he was excited. He had a slight intellectual disability and had a speech impediment.

Housekeeping on the ward was performed by the patients. Because of some of the patient's inability to walk long distances, or to walk at all, food on the ward was served in a small room adjoining one of the sleeping bays. The few capable patients on the ward took care of these duties. Primarily this was John, an older man that was mute, and young Andy. Andy was of little help because of his condition, but what he lacked in ability he made up for in enthusiasm. In return for these duties, the ward helpers received small favors, such as staying up late, extra coffee, and extra time to smoke.

Anything I asked John to do was answered with a toothless smile and, "I'd do anything for a tup of toffee!"

John also helped with the wheelchair and bedbound patients. If a patient messed his bed, John was right there, always smiling. When Ivan needed turned, his bed sores dressed or his bed made, John was there. He played catch with Andy by the hour with a small soft rubber football. He also helped with feeding the more helpless patients.

The relief came at 1:30 a.m. Usually the other ward helpers would be in bed by that time. but John would stay up and drink coffee and talk with me if I wasn't busy with nursing notes.

He remembered little to nothing of his past up to the point of his initially being picked up by the police, although occasionally something would surface from his past and surprise me. For example, once he heard the train that ran next to the hospital. He ran up to me and said, "I was on a twian once, Mr. Norith!" Smiling from ear to ear.

Sometimes, when we talked, I would question him, trying to find out a little about his past. Usually all I got was his confused smile. I would tell him we had to find out who he was so he could go home.

With a tiny sparkle in his eyes, he would tell me, "Thith ith my home, Mr. Norith!"

Let me tell you a little secret about hospitals of this type—and maybe all hospitals, for all I know. If a patient has no next of kin to protect his rights, he is a "ward of the state." The doctor can request the state to given permission for a certain therapy. The state assumes the doctor knows what he is talking about and usually approves it with no question. In principle, I suppose this is all right, although some doctors have used this for a reason to try experimental drug therapy, electroshock shock therapy, insulin shock therapy, and other procedures. Thankfully, lobotomies were never requested or performed at Clayton Memorial.

The doctors were determined they could get John's memory back. God only knows how many approved and unapproved experimental drug therapies were tried. He was just coming off his final round of experimental drug therapy when I came on the ward this particular night.

Sometimes he sang, or slept or talked to his private little demons, but I never remember seeing him violent. When a particular drug wore off, he would be the same old John.

The next thing they tried was insulin shock. In this treatment, the patient is given an overdose of insulin, and it is the Aide's responsibility to keep them up and walking around until it wears off, so they don't slip into a coma and die. This treatment wasn't popular with the doctors, and to my knowledge they only tried it on John once. It is a frightening thing to observe, and I hope I never have to see it again.

The next therapy was to be electroshock therapy. In those days, electroshock therapy was quite different than it is now. To perform the process, the temples are shaved and coated with conductive jelly. Next, electrodes are placed on each temple of the patient (who has by this time received a tranquilizer), and an electrical current is run between the electrodes. The current basically goes between the frontal lobes and the rest of the brain and effectively cuts off communications between these two areas. For reasons not clearly understood, at least by me, the patient loses the memories of the upper brain. He still has the functions of the lower brain, such as bodily functions, breathing, and that sort of thing; he just loses his memory.

The way I understand this, with the memories of past events that are blocking the patient's brain from functioning gone, the brain has a chance to function normally, and when the memory does come back, the patient can deal with whatever caused the problem in the first place.

Nowadays, the current is exceptionally low, the patient is conscious the whole time, and memory loss is minimal. In those days, things were quite different.

Then, six to twelve patients were taken to a room either voluntarily or involuntarily. They were slightly drugged that morning to make this process as painless as possible. They were strapped to a bed with their heads pointing to the center aisle. The doctor entered the room from one end. Next came a nurse pushing a cart with the instrument on it. Just before the patient was shocked, another drug was given to relax the nerves, and finally a piece of rubber, looking very much like the heel of a shoe, was placed in his mouth to keep the patient from breaking his teeth. Two Aides stood on each side of the patient. One Aide on each side restrained the patient by holding his upper arm and his wrist, and one Aide on each side restrained the patient by holding him just above the knee and the ankle.

The patient's temple would have been previously shaved and greased. The nurse placed the electrodes, which looked like an old-time pair of ice tongs, on the temples. The doctor pushed a button, driving the patient into convulsions so severe that if he weren't properly held (and occasionally when he was held properly), he could break his own bones. To give you an idea of the violence of this procedure, if an Aide were to have touched the electrodes and the patient at the same time the shock was applied, the shock would have killed both the Aide and the patient.

Upon completion of the treatment, the patient was unconscious for eight to ten hours. Once awakened, it took three to five days for the patient to recover any memory. The treatment was usually given as a series twice a week for a month or more.

Of course, the patients knew all this, and needless to say, were not too receptive to it. Bedlam usually ensued on treatment day until the candidates could be brought to the treatment room and strapped down.

But John was one of the quiet ones and sometimes tried to help others, especially when Andy had to go. When the procedure was over, I would try to be there when John woke up. I would ask him how he was.

"Where am I?" he invariably answered.

"You're home!" I always told him. He would smile his strange smile and either doze off again or get up and try to move around and get some coffee and a smoke.

The shock treatment didn't help, and finally they gave that up also. It didn't help Andy either. They just couldn't seem to get a handle on his seizures. Andy kept having his seizures and John kept acting like he just dropped out of the sky one day.

Then it was back to drug therapy, and that didn't help that time either. Sometimes it made him a little crazy and sometimes a little dopey, but when it was over, he was just plain John Doe, and he still made life a little more pleasant for all of us on the ward.

Then came that fatal night. All the patients were sleeping except for John. John had finished the ward housekeeping and was tossing Andy's toy football from hand to hand, smoking a cigarette. Smitty, my Aide, was checking sleeping areas and I was completing the nursing notes. John and I made small talk for a while, then sat in silence waiting for the relief. I glanced at the clock. It was 11:30 p.m., an hour and a half to shift change.

John made a small noise and I turned to ask him what he had said, just in time to see him slump to the floor. I leaped to his side and could see he wasn't breathing. I turned him over, elbows perpendicular to his body, and started artificial respiration. In those days, the person performing the artificial respiration sat with the patient's head between his knees and first pressed on the patient's lower chest just above the waist, and then lifted up where the upper arm joined the body. I yelled at Smitty to call security and get a doctor.

Smitty repeatedly called for help and kept the ward in order. Other patients were milling around trying to find out what happened. I could hear Ivan calling from his bed just around the corner. Andy stood there with tears running down his face, silently pleading with me to make things all right.

It was almost 12:30 a.m. before medical assistance arrived. The doctor checked him, then took me by the arm and pulled me away.

"It's all over," he said.

"No, no, he is going to be all right," I insisted, sweat running down my face.

But the medics put him on a gurney and took him away. We got things quieted down and the patients back to bed and the shift changed. I felt drained. Smitty and I sat in the lobby in the front of the building for a long time when we went off shift. We just didn't have the energy to walk back to the dorms.

Two months later I was transferred to another ward. I never saw the patients of the hospital ward again. Sometimes even today I wonder if anyone misses John Doe. I can't help but wonder if a mother or a child somewhere misses him. I know Andy does. I know I do.

The *General W. H. Gordon*

T HE *General W. H. Gordon* sits in San Diego harbor, gently bumping the dock. This will be her last year of plying the Pacific. She has sailed both the Pacific and the Atlantic and been in three wars. She has 11 awards, including three battle stars for Korea and two battle stars for Vietnam. She is 20,175 tons loaded, 662 feet 7 inches long, and has a 75-foot 6-inch beam. She has two steam turbines driving twin screws and is armed with both 20mm and 40mm guns as well as a 5-inch cannon on the fantail.

She has a crew of 43 officers and 464 enlisted men. She can carry 397 officers and 4,882 enlisted men to wherever she is told to take them. This trip will take Marines to Kobe, Japan.

The captain walks all compartments on the ship, checking to assure himself that the *Gordon* will make yet another trip across the Pacific. He has ultimate responsibility of his 506-man crew as well as the 5,279 passengers. The trip will take 18 days and the captain will not sleep for more than four hours at a time. If the weather turns bad, he may put a cot on the bridge so he will be closer to his ship.

With the Marines loaded, he departs to the open sea. As soon as he clears San Diego harbor, he sees the start of the predicted foul weather. The *Gordon* has weathered many storms, especially on the Atlantic, which is known to be rougher than the Pacific. The *Gordon* wallows in the rough waters. Crew members send the Marines on deck below to their designated compartments. Hatches are battened down as the water gets rougher.

Waves are now breaking over the bow and running down the deck to the fantail. Soon she is not just plowing through waves but riding over them. Before the night is over, she is struggling to get to the crest of the waves.

When she does reach the crest of a wave, she tips forward and the screws come out of the water. The ship shakes like a dog shaking a rat. She then plunges down the other side of the wave with a gut-clutching swoop, slams into the next wave as if she is going under, but then straightens and starts up the next wave. This goes on for five days and nights.

The rough seas and the constant smell of burning diesel make three-fourths of the Marines on board seasick and either vomiting or having dry heaves. They are forced to eat standing in case they suddenly feel their stomachs heave and must make a run for the nearest head (latrine). Many don't make it. Some go to the sick bay, and some try to settle their stomachs with soda crackers and weak tea. Nothing really helps. Those that prayed to get better at first now pray that God will let them die.

The Marines are amazed that they live to see Kobe. As they disembark, they stagger until they get used to being on solid ground. Many will never get seasick again. Some will be seasick as soon as they lose sight of land. Even some sailors that have spent years at sea will get seasick when the water turns rough. Some sailors will try to get shore duty, it is so bad, and they dread rough water so much.

To the captain, this is just another trip. He will be glad to get back to the States and his family. He is usually away from home one to two months at a time. He has captained ships for twenty years.

Two years later, most of the Marines on this trip will return home on a different ship, the *Patrick*. The water will be so calm on the trip back to the States it will seem like a pleasure cruise. Sunny days playing cards on deck, sleeping, and reading. Somctimes the passengers will see flying fish alongside the ship. Hardly anyone will be seasick. They will sit down to eat in the well-appointed mess hall. Thoughts of the *Gordon* will be nearly forgotten. However, the new ship and new captain will see it as just another trip across the ocean.

Windows to Another World

I am up early and hopefully having the house to myself. I sit in my favorite place under the window with my coffee and my newspaper. My peace is short-lived when my niece's little girl, Andrea, jumps in my lap, pulls the paper down, and kisses me.

"Tell me a story," she says.

"It's too early for stories," I tell her.

She pouts for a little bit and I try to get my paper in a position I can read it. In one leap the dog is in my lap vying for position and attention. This does not bode well for my plan for a quiet morning. I push the dog off, but she jumps right back up, nuzzling my hand to get me to pet her. Andrea is plotting her strategy to get attention also.

"Can we look at the windows book?" she asks.

I have always taught my children, nieces and nephews, and any child that would listen that photos are windows into another time and place. I tell them photos are the history of their lives, the lives of their loved ones, and the lives of their ancestors.

"Yes," I tell her. "Go get one of them."

I push the dog off again and point a finger at her telling her to stay.

Andrea is back with one of the older albums. She crawls back in my lap and opens the book in the middle. Andrea starts all books in the middle. One of the pictures is of her grandfather (my brother) sitting on the front bumper of a half-track with a big smile on his face. Pointing to him, I ask her "Who's that?" It's this game we play. We play it with numbers, colors, animals, and whatever.

"It's Uncle Howard," she says.

"Not Uncle Howard, you boob. That's your granddad Howard. Do you remember where I told you he was in that picture?"

Her little face scrunches up and she gives it some thought.

"Gokrea," she says.

"Not even close," I tell her. "Try again."

She looks at me, begging for a little help.

"Korea," I tell her. "What is he doing there?"

"He is a sojar," she says. I let that mispronounced word go as close enough.

He was hit right after that picture was taken. One time when we were drunk, he told me about it. The blood and the dirt in the aid station, and the medics and nurses struggling with exhaustion, and trying to decide who to look at next. Laying there for hours, the blood drying and sticking his uniform, and to his flesh.

I turn the page to get away from the memories. She points to a family picture of my dad's people. She points at my dad. He stands out in pictures.

"That's my daddy," I say. "He was your great grandpa."

"Where does he live?" she asks.

"He's in heaven with your great grandma," I tell her.

"Who's that?" she asks, pointing to another person.

"You know. You tell me." She ponders the problem for a while without speaking. You can almost hear the wheels turning in her little head. Then she claps her hands and says, "That's Aunt Gracie. She's in heaven too."

We turn a few more pages, both in our own thoughts, sometimes talking about other pictures. Finally, she stops my hand but doesn't say anything. I try to figure out what she is looking at. It's a picture of her and her mother.

"Who's that?" I ask her.

"That's me and my mama," she says.

"Go wake her up," I tell her.

I hear her mother grousing in the other room. So much for that idea. Andrea will want to look at pictures again, but I'm not in the mood now. The picture of her granddad Howard depressed me somehow.

When Andrea comes back, she sits beside me and dozes off. The dog is nowhere to be seen. I go back to my paper and coffee and the house slowly comes to life.

Montana Homestead

MILDRED was frightened. Her mother was large and ungainly, and she was sure the baby would come soon. The fear that followed her each time her mother became pregnant was with her again. The last pregnancy had been twins. The midwife had shooed the children and dad outside, where they huddled in the dark listening to her cries of pain.

After the twins were born, Mildred and dad had assumed the initial responsibility of caring for the babies. Her mother had watched with vacant eyes, sometimes asking to hold the babies, but never getting up from the bed.

The twins were puny, the smallest no larger than a kitten. On the second day that one had died. Dad had told Mildred to go to the neighbors and stay until he came for her. She had taken the boys and walked the four miles to the McClelland's.

The boys had asked her over and over what was wrong with mama, but she had no answer, so rather than lie to them, she told them nothing.

Three days later, Dad had come for them. She had looked into his face until he had to acknowledge her presence.

"Mama is OK," he had told her then. After a long pause he had said, "The second twin died also. Mama is very sad. We must all be very quiet and not disturb her."

When they reached their homestead, Dad had gone inside, and Mildred stayed outside with the boys.

The boys had gathered around her, four pleading little faces, waiting for her to say something. She had led them down to the corral and into the barn. Together they had crawled into the loft and sat huddled in a tight circle. She looked at them, one at a time. George, the oldest, was only seven. Don was just turning five.

Little Bill was too young to understand exactly what was going on, but had known that things were not right.

It was warm in the barn, out of the wind. She had looked at the boys and wondered where their lives would lead them. Would their lives become a succession of living on the edge of survival, or would one or all of them find a happier life?

"Mama is very sick," she had told them. "Your baby twin sisters are in heaven with God. Life was too hard here and God wanted them to have a better life."

Now Mama was nearly ready to have a new baby.

Mildred herself was only ten and already had the responsibilities of a grown woman. With the new baby coming, life would be even harder for her.

This time she told the boys the same thing she had told them before.

"We must be very quiet and help Dad," she said. "Mama is still very sad about the twins going to live with God. Also, she is sick from being ready to have a new baby."

Little Bill watched her with big eyes. He understood little of what she said, but if Mildred said it was a fact, then it was a fact. He would try to be a good boy, but wasn't sure exactly what he could do. He hoped that whatever he did made Mildred happy.

"We will all work together like we did when Mama had the twins. George, you and Don will have to do the outside work. There is wood and water to bring in and the stock must be looked after. I will help Dad take care of Mama and cook. Little Bill will help me with the dishes." As an afterthought she added, "We all must be very quiet."

"Can we talk to Mama?" little Bill asked. He had crawled over to Mildred and got in her lap. Tears were starting in his eyes and his little hands were digging into the soft flesh of her forearms.

"I want my Mama," he whimpered.

"It's OK, Bill," she said. "We will see if Dad will let you see Mama, but you must promise not to get in her lap, or cry or disturb her in any way."

"I will, I will," he said. "I will be a good boy. I will do anything you say to do, sissy. I just want to see my mommy."

They walked toward the house, Bill running ahead. George took Mildred's arm and held her back.

"Where are the twins?" he asked.

Mildred knew what he was asking. "They went to live with God," she said. She hoped that he would leave it there, but he had the curiosity of a child and it bothered him.

"Their bodies, I mean. After their souls went to heaven. Where are the bodies?"

Mildred did not have the remotest idea what Dad had done with the bodies. She also did not know what to tell George. "I don't know," she said. "Don't ask."

Mildred feared that Dad might have burned the little bodies in the stove. She knew this was not rational thinking, but in nightmares, she kept seeing Dad put them in the stove, like little sticks of wood. She had wanted to ask Dad so the terror would go away.

But she had never asked, and now it was all starting to happen again with the new baby.

Two days later, the McClellands brought Dad home in a wagon. They had been skidding logs for his new barn and the horses had bolted, dragging the skid of logs over his feet. The doctor came from Harlowtown and looked at the mangled feet.

"I don't think anything is broke, but his feet are a mess. He won't be working for a while. Soak them every night and rub them with the same salve you use on the cow's teats. Keep an eye on the toenails. If they get bad, I will come back up and remove them. Mostly, it is a matter of time. If he doesn't get infection in them, he will probably survive it all right."

Things went from bad to worse. Dad's feet swelled and turned black from the ruptured blood vessels. The pain was excruciating, keeping him from doing any of the work required around the homestead.

McClelland's children were too young to be of any help, though Jack McClelland himself came to their homestead, after a hard day's work, and tried to help as best he could. But the brunt of responsibility fell on Mildred's shoulders.

George helped direct the boys. Mildred managed to make it through each day, cooking for them all, cleaning, and seeing that all the things that had to be done were done.

Mama continued to grow larger and larger with the new baby. With Dad down with his damaged feet, Mama felt a need to help as much as she could and got out of bed occasionally.

Since the loss of the twins, Mama had been weak and irritable. She had also fallen into a deep depression. Not so much because of losing the twins, but because she somehow felt she had failed Dad. Now Dad needed her desperately and she was failing him again.

Dad, on the other hand, was in constant agonizing pain with his feet. They had finally quit swelling and some of the swelling had even diminished. He soaked them faithfully every night and rubbed the ointment he used on the cow's teats on his feet. He then would slip on old winter socks. If he were careful, he could scoot himself around backwards on his butt. He still couldn't stand, but he had been to the barn twice. The first time had taken him the better part of one afternoon. The Jersey had sustained a wire cut on her bag that had come infected and he felt that he must look at it. After treating the wound, he had carefully scooted himself across the yard and back to the house.

He worried extensively about his wife, Lulu. She appeared to not be getting any better. For hours at a time, she stared at the walls or out the small window. He wondered if she missed their home back in Rochester.

He thought of abandoning the homestead and moving to a more populated region. When he was better, he decided, he would find better place for them to live.

The crisis passed. The new baby was born fat and healthy. They named it Harold. Dad's feet got better. After more struggle, eventually they gave up the homestead in Montana and moved to Wyoming.

Author's Note

My mother Mildred told me this story from her childhood. Lulu, her mother, had many children, some of whom died as babies, as was common in those days. In the late 1800s, Lulu and her husband moved to Montana from Rochester, New York.

Cooke City Robbery

THE two peaks loomed in front of us in the cold morning light. Snow was falling in large lazy flakes.

"We will ride to where Lake Creek runs into the Clarks Fork of the Yellowstone, and then we will split up," Harrison informed us.

I felt uncomfortable around Harrison. There was no reason for him to kill the teller at the bank. Now we all had ropes waiting for us in Cooke City.

"The Swede goes with me," I told no one in particular. I was riding to the left of Harrison and slightly behind him. I would make damn sure to never get in front of him.

"I ride with Dale," the Swede confirmed. "You other three can go back over the mountain to Big Valley. Me and Dale will follow the Clarks Fork to Trout Creek and over Dead Indian summit to Cody."

"You'll do whatever I tell you," Harrison snapped at the Swede.

The Swede looked at him for a moment before he replied, "I'll do whatever I damn well please."

The Swede was also slightly behind Harrison. He had his coat pushed back, exposing his pistol. "We divide the money 'even' like we said," he told Harrison.

The other two looked at Harrison for confirmation. Harrison was looking off toward the Clarks Fork river. Pilot Peak and Index Peak were now behind us to our right, barely visible in the gently falling snow.

I don't know what Harrison's problem was. He was all buddy-buddy until the robbery, but now he was touchy and starting to get bossy.

Because I was behind him and I was sure he couldn't see me, I loosened my pistol in its holster.

I could see the Clarks Fork of the Yellowstone River ahead of us, which meant we weren't too far from Lake Creek.

"We'll stop at Lake Creek and split the money," Harrison informed us.

I was okay with that, as long as I had a clear view of Harrison and the other two. I didn't have a problem with the Swede, I just didn't want to put myself in a position that exposed me to Harrison and the other two.

"It's a lot of money," one of the other guys said. I think he was a relative of Harrison and his name was Bob or Rob or something like that. The fifth guy was Dennis Miller. I knew him from Red Lodge, Montana. He was an okay guy when he was sober, but a little unpredictable when he was drinking.

Things had gotten ugly at the bank after Harrison had shot the teller. People had started screaming and scrabbling to get out. I was blocking one door and Dennis was blocking the other door.

"Let's ride!" I hollered. The shooting was bound to bring the locals down on us. We were all candidates for a rope thanks to Harrison. The horses were tied behind the bank for easy access.

"Down! Down! Everybody down!" screamed Harrison. He signaled with his hand for the four of us to go. I was all too happy to get the hell out of there. The bank had become a death trap.

As we mounted the horses, I heard Harrison screaming again. "I'll kill the first person that raises their head."

I turned my horse and headed for Lake Creek, which was our rendezvous point. I looked back over my shoulder and saw Harrison heading away from the bank, shooting into the air.

Crazy bastard! I thought, but he turned down an alley and doubled back. Hopefully, any pursuit would not see him turn into the alley and double back.

It worked. No one seemed to notice him double back. It would buy us some time.

We all met at Lake Creek later to divide up the money.

"I should get a bigger share of the money. We wouldn't be here if I hadn't decoyed the posse," Harrison said.

"Yeah," the Swede told him, "We could have ridden quietly out of town if you hadn't shot the teller. Did you write your neck size on the wall so they would know what size of noose to make for you?"

I hadn't realized how mad the Swede was. Things were getting more complicated by the minute.

"Just divide up the money, split up, and ride," I told them. I wanted to ride in the river downstream as far as possible in case there were dogs after us. I hoped the Swede would come with me. He was the only one in the whole group I felt comfortable around now.

I watched as Harrison set the money out in five piles. When he was done, I grabbed a pile and stuffed it in my saddle bags. I put my left foot in the stirrup, but a cold voice stopped me. I turned.

Harrison had a pistol in his hand. "Get down!" he told me. "Untie your saddle bags and toss them over here."

Damn! I had gotten so interested in the money I had taken my eyes off Harrison. The Swede, still on the ground, backed slowly toward his horse.

"Stay out of this, you ignorant Scandinavian," Harrison told the Swede.

Harrison had made two bad errors of judgement. First the Swede was fast. He already had his pistol in his hand and was pointing it at Harrison. Second, the Swede didn't mind killing Harrison or anybody else if it was necessary.

"We're done here. Get your two sidekicks and ride. Don't look back," the Swede told Harrison.

There they were. Each with pistols pointed at each other. Suddenly the Swede shot Harrison.

"What the hell?" I said.

"It was in his eyes," the Swede said. "He was just a heartbeat away of killing both of us."

The other two stood there, watching the Swede closely. I could see the fear in their eyes.

"Drag him back in the bushes. We'll split his share. Unless you two want a little of the action Harrison got," the Swede said softly. He was clearly in control.

I didn't know where I stood. I had my hand on the butt of my pistol. Things were very tense.

"We will go as planned," the Swede said. "You two go back over the pass to Red Lodge, and Dale and I will follow the Clarks Fork to Trout Creek and go over Dead Indian Pass into Cody. From this moment on, I don't know you guys and have never seen you before, and you have never seen me or Dale."

They nodded. After a feeble attempt to hide Harrison, they turned and followed Lake Creek upstream. The Swede and I went down to the Clarks Fork and started riding downstream in the water.

In the distance I could hear dogs baying.

Fear

CALIFORNIA'S west coast is marked by the mighty Pacific Ocean, the largest body of water in the world. At times, especially at low tide, the water is so calm it appears a person could walk on it. At other times, long, low waves lap the shore, to the delight of surfers. On yet other times, howling winds drive the waves to unimaginable heights, topped by vicious white caps.

I knew better than to take my little boat, with its marginal Gray Marine engine, out as far as I did. I also knew better than to take my two passengers, especially the boy, but I was after the big fish known to live where the continental shelf drops off to the abyss of the ocean floor.

Near Santa Cruz, California just south of San Francisco, is arguably the best fishing anywhere.

This is where we found ourselves. We had beer, sodas, and plenty of food. The sun beat down, the fishing was great, and the three of us dozed in the soft warmth and the gentle rolling of the sea. We were wakened by a hard rain squall and a heaving ocean.

Even though just a little bit drunk from the beer, I could still see this could turn into a bad situation. Drowning is my worst fear. Then being attacked by wild animals (sharks in this case). In tough situations like this, you need to keep your wits about you. Your only hope of surviving is to keep the boat's bow into the wind and hope the motor doesn't die.

Fear suddenly grips me. Is there time to make a sea anchor if the engine dies? What could I make it out of? Do I dare leave the ship's controls to find out? If the boat goes down, what can I salvage that will help keep us afloat? I ask myself these questions, hoping an answer will come to my mind.

Think think think, I tell myself. Fear grips my stomach and makes me weak. The fear causes my brain to go blank. I struggle to force myself to think. If we are lost out here, how much water is aboard? How much food is aboard? are my next questions. The wind is blowing from the east, so we will be drifting further and further out to sea if the motor dies. My friend, David, the Englishman from work, and Danny, the neighbor's fatherless boy and my constant companion, are both pale with fear. Which one is going to crack first and become part of the problem? I must reassure them somehow, and I don't believe I can talk without becoming hysterical myself.

I call them both forward. "OK," I tell them. "This could get ugly. David, I want you to stay toward the back of the boat. Move back and forth from the cabin to the stern as is necessary to keep the bow slightly high. And keep the can of ether handy in case the engine dies."

The boy is in the small cabin beside me. I take him by the upper arm.

"Danny," I tell him, "I have to take the waves at a forty-five degree angle so we won't get swamped. I have to watch the water. I want you to stand just behind the cabin and keep an eye out for land. Keep me informed so we are going the right direction." This is just a busy work job for him, but I want to keep his mind occupied.

I pat the kid's shoulder, point to the little bit of land we can see and smile at him. I'm sure he can't tell I'm crying because my tears are mixed with sea spray.

I fight the boat to keep going toward land at a forty-degree angle. Occasionally I reach back and pat the kid on the leg. He is a real trooper, and I am proud of him. Finally, after what seems like a lifetime, we appear to be approaching the beach.

We are further north of Santa Cruz beach than I originally thought, because I can't see any harbor, only sand. I call the Englishman forward to give him and the boy their final instructions.

"I'm going to beach the boat. When I do, the boat may turn sideways in the surf. If it does, it will roll." I swallow the bile in my throat. Please God don't let that happen, I think. I continue, "As soon as we hit the sand, have the bow line in your hand and get out of the boat. Get away from the boat quickly so you don't get trapped inside if it rolls. When you are clear, pull the boat up on the sand with the bow line as far as you can. I'll go to the stern so the bow will rise up to help you out a little." I put David and Danny on each side of me directly behind cabin. I'm resorting to praying by this time, begging God.

I tell them, "I'll try to turn perpendicular to the beach at the last moment."

As I come closer, I start getting the boat into position. I look back at my friends. I tell them, "This is it." We do a quick heads up, then the time has come.

I turn the bow directly toward the beach and slowly advance the throttle until the little Gray Marine engine is screaming. I realize I am screaming with it. "Please don't die now!" I tell the engine.

The next thing I know, the beach looms before me. I don't have time to change my mind. We're beached.

I move to the fantail until I can see the boat is well up on the beach. Then I move aft to get out of the boat. The Englishman and the kid are out of the boat, but are still in waist-deep water. I jump over the side and the three of us pull the boat further up on the sand with the bow line.

It is suddenly over, and all three of us are shaking, and sitting on the beach, laughing and crying at the same time.

Silently I whisper a little prayer thanking God.

The Psychic Healer

As told by Deannie Kelly

F OR many years I confided this story to only my closest friends, for fear people would not believe me or might even ridicule me or accuse me of outright story telling.

Almost everyone has heard tales of psychic healing. Many are skeptical or downright disbelieving. I would like to tell a true story, that happened to me personally, concerning psychic healing in the Philippines. Please keep an open mind and save your conclusions until you have read the whole story.

First, let me explain what led me to seek a psychic healer. When I was about twenty-three years of age, I started having health issues. The first symptoms occurred when I ate. As soon as I swallowed food, I had severe pain in my chest area and my stomach.

The doctors tried various treatments, mostly for ulcers. This went on for about three years.

The doctors did more surgeries, removing parts of my intestines each time. I was in and out of hospitals for different surgeries and treatment for the next two years.

At this time, my brother-in-law was in the hospital in Salt Lake City, Utah, for open heart surgery. While he was there, he was telling his doctor, a cardiologist, about me and how skinny I was getting. The doctor said, "My God, she has Crohn's disease!" He had never even seen me! But he knew. He told my brother-in-law that one of the best doctors for Crohn's disease was at the University Hospital, right there in Salt Lake City, Utah.

He made me an appointment. When I called the hospital, the doctor that talked to me said, "We got it all set up, all you have to do is come in." I went to the University Hospital and in ten days they ran all kinds of tests on me.

They decided it was Crohn's Disease. If I had never been operated on and would have gone to the right doctors to start with, they would have treated it and it could have been controlled. Once you have surgery, and you have been given an anesthesia, it tends to make the disease flare up.

To this day, doctors are not sure what causes Crohn's disease. You inherit the genes, but that does not mean that anyone in your family has had it.

It's kind of lying dormant in your body and then all a suddenly it appears. You never had any problems with your tummy or your digestive system or anything until then.

When I was little, one or two, until I started school, maybe the second or third grade I was a quite chubby kid. I was never thin, and I was able to eat everything. I never had any problems that I recall.

Doctors told me, on somebody like me, because my mother didn't have it, but my mother had an aunt or uncle that had it, they could have been a carrier. and I could have got it that way. Mostly it would show up in puberty, from ages 10 or 11 to the early twenties. If you're going to get it, that's when you usually get it.

Well, in those days, they didn't know. Consumption is what they called it. They had a belly ache, or appendicitis, they just died because their stomach hurt. He said that could have happened. What happens with Crohn's is, like me, my intestines broke and I got peritonitis and stuff. The problem in a lot of women is, if you get pregnant and you have Crohn's, when the womb starts to enlarge, it pushes against the intestines and it can form a fistula right into the womb and it kills you and the baby. That could happen even before thcy would know you were pregnant. So, when they found out I had it, they told me I could never, never have children again because of it.

When I first got it in the early seventies, the doctors told me that they rarely saw it out of medical school. Now, it's not that uncommon. What happens with Crohn's is you get ulcers inside the intestines. The ulcers heal and it becomes like a scar. The outside of the intestine stays the same, but the inside gets smaller and smaller. Then it flares up and you get the ulcers again, and again and again until the insides of the intestines get so tiny that nothing solid can pass through it. So, the waste must liquefy itself before it can pass through. Once it starts forming the scars from those ulcers, the intestines can't absorb any vitamins or nutrients from the food you eat.

In 1979, I got sick again. I was having a lot of trouble, with pain mostly. I went to the hospital and they ran a bunch of tests and decided the two and a half foot of intestine that had been bad for past two years, had gotten to the point where it needed worked on again. When they got through, I was in the hospital for thirty days. My food transit time was seven minutes.

My sister, Bobby, lived in Alaska then. Bobby knew about a US Senator whose daughter had been to the Philippines to see psychic healers. A lot of people in Alaska go to them. Bobby had learned the Senator's daughter had Crohn's disease too. The daughter periodically went to the faith healers in the Philippines, and she gets along quite well.

The daughter told Bobby about a man known as Doctor Tony, who was in Baguio, the Philippines. He was thought to be one of the better psychic healers there. There are a lot of psychic healers, but you must be careful because some of them are just out for the money. We were told if they accept money, you don't go to them because they aren't for real. We decided that, for lack of not knowing what else to do, we should go to Doctor Tony.

We planned through a tour company that provided this service specifically. The name of the company was Around the World Tours. They took people to the Philippines to the faith healers.

Bobby and I decided to go. We were gone for thirteen days.

After arriving in Baguio, we went to the hotel our guide had arranged for us to stay in. There were a lot of Swiss and German and Japanese people there that had been sent by their doctors to see Doctor Tony.

The only thing that they ask you to pay for is the hotel where you stay. The hotel staff asked that you go to a sort of religious service daily. You go into this room and sit on mats. They also have you do a mantra that is to teach you to relax. They said that they also read your aura.

After you do this every morning for half an hour, you go over to a building on the grounds where Doctor Tony's office was. You sit in a waiting room, just like any doctor's office. Then when you went into his exam room, he had a table you could lay on. Dr. Tony never asked you what was wrong with you, nor did anyone at the tour company or in the Philippines. No one was aware I had Crohn's disease. All they knew was you were going over there to see them about a health issue.

When we went in, the first day there, Doctor Tony has you lay on this table. It's like an examining table, but it is just one long flat table. He takes his hands and puts them together and then he holds them maybe three or four inches off your body. He goes from your feet up in a circular motion all over your whole body and when he gets up to your head he stops. Then he went right back to my side. The Crohn's is in my lower right side.

He said, "This is where your problem is at."

I was laying there, and I was quite tense and nervous, and I was thinking, "Whatever he is going to do is really going to hurt." I was scared. I never knew what a psychic healer did.

He spoke only broken English. He really doesn't talk to you that much. He told me he had never been to the United States. He also told me, "I know you are afraid, but I am not going to hurt you." He said, "I want you to see what I am doing." So he had his nurse get a mirror and hold it above me. He was moving his hands around and my body started to get warm. It was like putting a heating pad or a hot water bottle on yourself somewhere. Suddenly, he wiggled his fingers, and I could feel his fingers were inside of me. He didn't cut me. He told me he believed that if you concentrate enough, you can use your mind to separate the cells and that is how they take care of you. He put his fingers in and removed adhesions. The doctors in Salt Lake had told me that I had a lot of pain adhesions, but there was nothing they could do about it. They didn't want to go back in and operate again because of the problems I had with anesthetics. Dr. Tony went in and he removed a lot of the adhesions.

While I was laying there, and Doctor Tony had his fingers inside of me, he had me put my hand in a bowl, and I'm assuming it was like rubbing alcohol. He dipped my fingers in liquid. Then he had me stick my fingers down in this hole. I was watching in the mirror and I could see my fingers go into my body. I could feel them. I could wiggle them around in there. There is a tiny bit of blood, I mean it barely ran over my side. But it was not like there was a massive amount of blood. He treated us like this for ten or fifteen minutes a day.

He never treated me in the same place on my body. He mostly went into the side or the stomach where he went in the first time when he was removing those pieces of adhesions. That was my biggest problem at the time. He tried to tell me what he was doing but I couldn't always understand him.

Every day when he got through it hurt a little bit less.

Before I left the Philippines, I was eating everything. They are big on fruit and vegetables. I was eating a lot of those. They are hard to digest. When I left home, I hadn't been eating things like this at all. All I could have was liquid stuff at home. When I left Alaska to go to the Philippines, I couldn't even eat solid food. There was no way I could keep it down. It went straight through me.

The very last day, Doctor Tony did my yin and yang. And that was painful. Really painful. That was the only thing that he did that hurt me.

They have one male nurse up by your head and one male nurse down by your feet.

It's like the male nurse at my feet was massaging my toes. Then suddenly, I got this terrible pain and it's not like he was squeezing your toes. I don't know what he does. Suddenly, I would get these sharp pains in my head. The other male nurse would put his hands there and it would go away. They said now that they had my yin and yang in harmony, it would be OK. The pain went away. I mean it just lasted a second when they did it. I've got along great since then. The doctors in the United States haven't operated on me for Crohn's since I left the Philippines.

I haven't had a lot of trouble with Crohn's disease until about the last year and a half. Now I'm getting worse again. I've never been back to see Doctor Tony.

Nowadays, the Philippines are not big on Americans. It is not as safe as when I went over there. When I went over there, they really liked Americans.

I had a friend that was a surgeon, and he said, "They have things in their sleeves. That was just parts of chickens that they were pulling out of you."

But I know it wasn't because my sister and I stood right beside each other. If they were working on her I would stand right beside her, and if they were working on me, she would stand there.

Doctor Tony was not very tall. He was probably not as tall as me and I am five foot three. He was nice, and he was always happy and smiling. He had dark hair. I would say he was around his late thirties or early forties. He always wore short-sleeved shirts with jungle designs on them. He was always very careful to wash his hands and arms before he treated you.

There was no one around the table except him. His nurses were men. They always wore short-sleeved shirts also. Whenever he removed anything from me when he was working on me, they would stand behind him and to the side. They couldn't have touched my body. He put the mirror over me every time he worked on me. He did that so I would be aware of what he was doing.

The male nurses would hand him the pan to wash his hands in. When he put his fingers in there and pulled out those pieces of adhesions out of my body, they held the bowl and he put pieces in it.

He showed me the bowl when they were through. Having been raised on a ranch, I know those were like chunks of gristle. I know they came from inside me because the bowl was empty when the nurses handed it to him. One nurse would stand and hold the mirror above my head and the other would stand by Doctor Tony.

The bowl would be empty when I was going up to get on the table. He would pick it up and he would kind of stand back and hold it out to Doctor Tony whenever he needed it. They never gave you anything to eat, so I know they weren't drugging me in any way.

He said one time he had told some people about his ability and accepted money because he thought he could build him a better healing center and stuff. So he accepted money and lost the ability to heal. For several years he couldn't do anything at all.

The healing center was up in the mountains. Only people that were going to be treated by Doctor Tony were there. He was booked all the time. I guess the Swiss and the German doctors sent their people to him a lot. There were many that came up there in big busses. Must have been twenty or thirty of them. The hotel was not big. Maybe they had thirty or forty rooms. It was a two-story building, and it was full all the time. There were few Americans there. With the tour guide, there were twelve of us Americans.

Doctor Tony didn't get money. He didn't live there at the hotel. You pay for the hotel, but as far as him there was never money exchanged. He lived in the town and he would come up to his clinic.

He never left marks on the body. I never found any marks on my body after I left his office.

When he would get through, he took his hands out of my body and I got this warm sensation. He would pass his hand over the top of where he had been working. He would pull his hands out and kind of swipe with his fingers over the area that had been open and suddenly the opening was gone. I would have little dribbles of blood on my side. The nurse would wipe it up with a cloth. Then he would have you go to your room and lie down. He said anytime you disturbed the cell structure of the body, it causes trauma, and you need to rest and relax. So he asked that you go back to your room and lie down.

You felt tired, but there was never any pain. There were never any marks. You couldn't see where he had done it.

I have the pictures of him doing it. When he did it to my sister, my sister had bad headaches. She had them for an exceptionally long period of time. They weren't like migraine headaches; they were just real bad headaches. Our mother had taken her to several doctors, and they had told her at one time that the blood vessels going into the back of her head were too small and that is what caused the pain. So, while she was there with me, she decided to have Doctor Tony look at her. He had her lay on her belly with her head up to the front of the table. He took his fingers and was massaging along the base of her skull, and he stopped right there on her side in the back.

He came to where the spine is at in the back of her neck, just kind of rubbing and suddenly, he just lifted his hand up. He had this black thing, I can only describe as kind of a spider or something, it was about the size of a quarter. It had long fingers like string. and he pulled them out and put it in the dish the nurse held. Then he rubbed his hand back over her head and her neck, and the hole was gone.

I have pictures of him with his fingers in her. He also worked on my back where I have a curvature of the spine. He went in there and worked on my back one day and it really helped for a long time. But he told me at that time because of the amount of time that my back had been that way that I needed to come back because he couldn't do it all at one time. He said you must come back again. And maybe again after that. I never did go back. He made my stomach better and that is what I went for. My back at that time was a minor thing.

My sister doesn't have headaches anymore at all. Her headaches went away.

There was a lady there that had cancer. She had chemo; she didn't have any hair. Instead of wigs, she wore a turban all the time. She and her mother were there because the doctors had told her that she only had six months to live. There wasn't any more they could do for her, they had done chemo and radiation and there just wasn't anything else they could do for her. I don't know how Doctor Tony treated her because I was never in the room when she was treated. She could just barely function. Before we left the Philippines, we went to Manila and spent a couple of days there.

She and I went down by the sea, she was that much better, that fast.

I know she was alive after that because when we came back to the United States, for a long time, Bobbie and I wrote to some of the people who were over there with us to see how they were doing. I felt better, but I wanted to know in my own mind that these other people were OK too. But they stayed OK. We kept in contact with them for a year or two afterward. Then I stopped. But they were all doing much better.

Someone told me that Doctor Tony had come over to the United States. He came over here and either went to Harvard or Yale or some school like that and did a lecture for them. They invited him to teach them about it. And after he had showed them, they wouldn't disagree with what he did, but they wouldn't say "Yes, what you're doing is right."

But I understand that he does come to the US. My sister told me. She told me that she heard that he came here, and there was a place in Montana that he went to, also.

They said that Doctor Tony's wife was very wealthy, and he came from a very wealthy family. Money was not a problem.

He didn't have to do it. There was no reason that he had to do it. But we did ask him when he found out he could do this. He said that when he was young something had happened to a friend of his and he said that's when he found out he could do it.

The last day we were in Baguio, we went to his wife's house to a "tea." We went and it was like a very formal English thing. I was surprised. The house was large and that was amazing, because over there these people did not have big houses. Some of them don't even have houses. They had like a stucco fence around it. It had gates and a guard. We went in and they had a carport that you pulled into by the front door. We went in and it was very American inside. It was a beautiful home. The furniture was very American. It was beautifully furnished. We just had a very formal tea. She served us out of silver. We sat, and we had little china cups. We had little cakes.

She didn't speak good English. But she was a very prim and proper lady. She was just as nice as she could be about the whole thing. She looked like she was in her early thirties, but we had a tour guide, and she was in her early twenties and when we asked her, she giggled and said she was thirty-eight. I would have sworn she was twenty. So, you know, it's hard to say. She didn't look close to middle age.

This story is true. Satisfy your curiosity and follow up on it. Keep an open mind is all I ask of you.

Author's Note

Doctor Tony's name was Antonio C. Agpaoa (1939–1982). The reader can find more information by searching for his name on the internet. One of the first results will be Wikipedia. Searching for "faith healers" or "psychic healers" will provide further information. If you are interested in finding out more about the debilitating effects of Crohn's disease, I also suggest the internet. The Crohn's and Colitis Foundation is worth looking into; their website is https://www.crohnscolitisfoundation.org/.